MARTINIS At Midnight

A Collection of
Intuitive Thoughts
and Recipes for
the Consummate
Martini Lover

by Marjie Martini

Note for the Librarians: A cataloguing record for this book is available from the Library and Archives Canada at www.collectionscanada.ca/amicus/index-e.html

ISBN 978-1-4303-0066-3

In memory of Clifford Cheales:
a man who loved a dry vodka martini
and loved to laugh even more.

Con

tents

To the readers:

I believe there are two consistencies in people's lives.

The first being a love for some kind of alcoholic beverage. It is the most common vice in the world and definitely the most socially acceptable.

The second being relationships. Whether you are in one, or wishing you had one, or you just got out of the relationship from hell, they are one of the most discussed issues in our lives.

My favorite vice is the martini. Forget beer or wine. My mother always said, "if you're going to drink, don't drink a lot, just make it count." A martini is very much like a relationship: mix a few essentials together, shake or stir it up and the results are always surprising.

"Martinis at Midnight" evolved out of my desire to help people better understand their lives; and their need to realize that the best solution to any problem is a good laugh. When friends get together and share a martini it is a time for them to let the stresses of life go. Life is all about balance and when people share experiences and laughter it helps level out all the other craziness of our lives.

I hope you enjoy and share this collection of stories and recipes with others. These are my insights into how martinis and relationships make us laugh, cry and hopefully give us clarity. For more entertaining stories and fabulous recipes, check out ***www.martinisatmidnight.com***.

Marjie Martini

About Marjie Martini

This letter was submitted by Marjie's loving girlfriends.

You know that girl who you see at the Martini bar, who is having way too much fun with her group of friends, the kind of fun you wish you were having?

> ...*That's Marjie Martini*

You know that girl with a certain flare, who is always dressed for fun?

> ...*That's Marjie Martini*

You know the girl who is always laughing and consistently has some crazy story or saga?

> ...*That's Marjie Martini*

Marjie has spent 10 years in a resort town cultivating the perfect martini. Her years as a hair stylist have dubbed her the "Hair Therapist." Great bartenders and fabulous hair stylists are the best sounding-boards for people's trials and tribulations. It always interested her that people's experiences were usually shared over some kind of beverage. Marjie started drinking martini's long before they were hip, when martini lists did not exist and good glasses were few and far between. She has spent the past decade surrounding herself with

"Top shelf friends and Top shelf martinis"

Her friends, both male and female, have been a source of inspiration and endless humour. There has always been some great story to be retold and the retelling has never begun until the chilled martini glasses are set in front of them. Her friends, she keeps in high regard, because without them, her life lessons would have been much harder and not nearly as entertaining.

Marjie will continue to find great humor in this thing called "life" and unbelievable joy and delight in every martini that crosses her lips. Her goal is to go skidding into her grave, martini in one hand, telephone in the other, laughing so hard that they have to slam the box shut to drown out her cackle. Can you think of a better way to conclude your life?

Signed
The Martini Girls

What you need to know about the recipes

It's only natural to feel like a geek at a party if you don't have the first clue about mixing a cocktail. Even professionals measure their ingredients. Don't guess to make a perfect drink every time. The following tips should give you a quick start to serving it up like "the hostess with the mostess" or the "host with the most".

Measures:	Pony = 1 oz
One Normal Shot Glass = 1oz.	Dash = 1/6 oz
Jigger = 1.5 oz-2 oz	Teaspoon = 1/8 oz

- Serve cocktails icy cold! Pre-chill glasses in the refrigerator or let them sit in shaved ice before using. Chilling makes drinks tastier!

- Always put ice in the shaker before pouring ingredients. That way, the liquids are chilled as they are poured over ice.

- You'll get more juice from lemons and oranges if you soak them in warm water.

- When the recipe calls for a twist of lemon peel, rub a narrow strip of peel around the rim of the glass. Then twist the peel so that one small drop will go into the drink. Then drop the peel.

- When the recipe consists of clear liquids, always STIR!

- If the recipes contains a carbonated liquid (soda, ginger ale), stir gently to preserve the bubbly! Stirring avoids blowing the top off the shaker.

- SHAKE drinks that contain fruit juices, sugar, eggs, cream or other ingredients that are difficult to mix. Really give it a good SHAKE - don't just rock!

- A clean piece of wax paper rubbed on the rim of a bottle will prevent dripping when you pour!

- For a "sugar-frosted" glass, moisten the rim of a pre-chilled glass with lemon or lime and then dip into powdered sugar (before alcohol is poured).

- When you shake a drink that requires an egg, use an ice cube. The cube breaks up the egg and helps it blend into the drink.

- Infusing: add the required fruit/nuts/spice to the selected alcohol and infuse for 2-7 days. The longer the ingredients sit, the stronger the favours will be.

- When a recipe calls for a wedge of lime or lemon cut fruit in ½ inch thick slices. Make a small cut in the center of the wedge, so that the slice will sit on the edge of the glass.

7 Signature Martinis

On this particular night, I was perplexed by the irony of life and by my indecision in choosing the perfect liquid concoction. Tonight, I was craving a little sweetness, which I could savor into the night. Cruising the martini menu is a lot like looking into the fridge, not knowing what you want, not knowing what you are looking for. After much contemplation, I decided that the Anti-Climactic Martini was my choice. Raspberry Vodka shaken with Chambord gives this martini just the right amount of sweetness. The splash of cranberry gives just enough tartness to the finish that makes this martini perfectly bittersweet. I was impressed by the Anti-Climactic presentation: the frosted glass and cranberry garnish made it very pretty, and I like pretty.

Just as my martini arrived so did my lovely male companion. (I refer to him as "companion" because "friend" doesn't include all the realms of our relationship, and "date" is overkill) The definition of a male companion, by the way is: a man who is definitely into you, calls you, takes you out, cooks you dinner, and cuddles with you but will not kiss you or cross the line into intimacy. The question is: "Is a companion a man who is possibly in denial about being gay?"

As usual, I get the long and tender hug when he arrives, then we settle into our discussion and debates of the trials and tribulations of our lives. The conversation is always stimulating and enticing. As I am sipping my martini, I realize my companion is

"The Perfect Date."

He is a true gentleman, who is handsome, interesting and flirtatious. However, there is an intrigue about my companion. Would the flirtation ever materialize into anything sexual? Would I ever get some or was I destined to end the perfect date with a peck on the cheek?

As the evening unfolds, he poses the question: "Would you like to go back to my house for dessert?" Needless to say, I said "Yes." After dessert, I was propositioned to go upstairs and cuddle? I quickly pick my jaw up off the ground and nodded because my brain was in disbelief that my companion had finally made his move. When he mentioned dessert, I thought that it was going to be edible, not sexual.

During foreplay, he whispers how first he is going to satisfy me many times. I was in ecstasy. How could I have thought that this man was gay? My gaydar must have been off. A few minutes later, I am stunned with the sensation of wetness. His wetness! Noooooooooo! Not a preemie! I am speechless. After all this, a preemie!! The room was heavy with embarrassment. As he leaves, all I can think is ....poor guy.

Conclusion:

As always, great insight comes to me in the latest hour of the evening. As I looked into my fridge for something satisfying, I realized that I needed to make myself another Anti-Climactic martini because something had to kill the frustration that was pulsating through my body. I took a long swig of the martini and a thought occurred: the sweetness of the raspberry is like the sweet teasing of hugging, cuddling and spooning with my companion, and the bittersweet cranberry finish is like the preemie, the bitter shock of reality. Unfortunately, both the Anti-Climactic martini and the companion always leave you wanting more!!

"Keep it simple:
Shake it, Pour it, Drink it"

Derek Jarman
King Martini Taster

The Anti-Climactic Martini

Recipe:

1 ½ oz. Raspberry Vodka

½ oz. Chambord

2 oz. cranberry juice

Shaken and strained into a chilled martini glass.

Garnished with a few cranberries.

*I*nsight has come to me, not late this evening but early this morning. I am writing this lying on the floor with my legs perpendicular to the wall. "Why, do you ask?" Not because of my amazing flexibility but as a result of the Raver Girl Martini and the activities associated after it, earlier this evening. You will never find this martini on any bar or restaurant list. This martini comes directly from my very dear friend, Raoul, bartender extraordinaire! (I call him Raoul to protect his privacy.) Besides, aren't all bartenders named Jack or Jo? Raoul and I go back many years and of course, many martinis.

One of Raoul's favorite things is to see chicks dance, (clothed and shaking it with no poles involved... not what you where thinking.) so he created

"A martini that makes a woman dance all night long."

The Raver Girl martini is a unique combination of Mandarin Vodka and Cointreau. Which you would think is too much orange but cut with BASE energy drink, a splash of 7-up and garnish this baby with a slice of orange, you are grooving for the rest of the evening! (For all those Red Bull enthusiasts reading this column, NO! you cannot use Red Bull. Raoul says, "It is just not the same.") As he is the martini artist, I have to agree. This martini surprises you: it comes out tasting like the old 80's candy Sweet/Tarts. This martini was fitting

considering, on this evening I was out with one of my lovely girlfriends, "Wilemina," who is very sweet but given enough martinis, can be quite the tart!

My friend is one of those girls who really hasn't experienced life to its fullest. We all know someone like her, a girl who grew up way too fast, is old before her time and who has always been too responsible. She usually comes from some kind of stifling or religious upbringing. Where having fun was bad or just not allowed. It is actually ironic that we are friends. I'd like to think we stretch each others' boundaries. She also has a lot of preconceived ideas about things she has not experienced, like a Rave! She, like many people, assumed that a Rave is a bunch of kids, tripped out on drugs, dancing to weird music, to all hours of the morning. While I am not denying this happens, on this particular evening, it was not the case.

There is a point in everyone's life where the stress and pressure becomes so great that all you want to do is curl up into a ball and hide; we reach the point of a breakdown. Now, we all do things to offset this stress; some people drink, others do drugs, some pop anti-depressants and some just crack. My solution? Dance!

Dancing is the most primitive form of self expression. All cultures do it; even our ancestors did it. Across the world dancing is always done

6

at life's milestones: birth, marriage and in some cultures, death. One recent form of dancing is the Rave. My personal definition of a Rave is a gathering of souls, where age, sex, color, religion, body shape, and social status are irrelevant. This gathering is a musical form of self expression, in which everyone is equal and nothing matters except the feeling of moving your body to the beat for as long as you need to, to release the stresses of the outside world.

On this evening, we ended up having a few of Raoul's martinis and by fluke, found our way to a Rave. Successfully convincing Wilemina to join the rave was a miracle. I swear, the moon and stars were in alignment on this evening, because she found herself in a room were she knew no one and it did not matter who she was. I watched in amazement as my pent up girlfriend let herself go. She was sweet and played the role of the tarty flirt but what hit me was that she was actually living in the moment and having fun! She was not conforming to society as she traditionally does. She was expressing herself and loving every minute of it. I just smiled and giggled as I took a sip of my Raver Girl martini and watched her dance the night away.

Conclusion:

I walked home barefoot with my girlfriend, heels in hand. She babbled on about how she was so

wrong about Raves and that she had never danced so much and had so much fun. She giggled when she said that she had never experienced such amazing music. I thought to myself that she is just like the Raver Girl martini; she is sweet and naïve most of the time, but given enough stress, and enough martinis, she becomes the tart, who wants to experience everything in one night. Thanks to Raoul and the Raver Girl martini we experienced one of those celebrations of life.

"Martinis are like every
good girl that secretly
wants to be a bad girl"

Gerry Porter
Server

The Raver Girl Martini

Recipe:

1 ½ oz. Mandarin Vodka

½ oz. Cointreau

2 oz. BASE energy drink

Splash of 7-up

Mix these ingredients together with ice.

Shake and strain into a chilled martini glass.

Garnish with an orange rind.

This particular evening was very mellow; it consisted of great food and very interesting conversation. The discussion was so stimulating that my girlfriend and I asked the bartender to create a martini that went with our chat. This was how the Dilemma martini was born. The situation was very serious, so I requested that the martini be strong. I needed its strength to digest the dilemma my girlfriend had laid before me.

Our bartender did a fabulous job creating a new recipe. My girlfriend loves gin, so including it, was the only stipulation. He created a martini with Gin, Grand Marnier, orange juice and a splash of lemon and lime. This martini was shaken and garnished with a lime wedge.

As I took my tentative first sip, I realized that our new bartender was fantastic. He definitely knew his stuff. I also realized that this martini would require another sampling. The Dilemma was strong but adding Grand Marnier cut the edge of the gin perfectly. After a few quick sips, my girlfriend began unraveling the tale of every woman's worst nightmare:

"How did I end up fooling around with a married man?"

I was shocked by her confession because I would classify her as "Miss Morality". I never would have thought this woman would cross that line. I needed to have another sip or two when she told me the affair was with her long term married friend. I ordered our second martinis, as she was describing the events of the previous evening. At this point she completely berated herself for ending up in this situation.

This individual had been in pursuit of my girlfriend for quite some time. She knew it, but enjoyed what she thought was harmless flirtation and flattery. However, the night before the flirtation became more racy and assertive, as this gentleman consumed several cocktails. The night concluded at her place. After several make out sessions, each interrupted by "What about your wife?" She came to her senses and asked him to leave. When she realized that she was not going to have sex with him and was really really horny she kicked him out in order to take care of herself. You have got to love a woman who understands her needs and owns a vibrator. As I ordered our third martini, I realized I liked this martini because it was robust but the lemon and lime made it very fresh and pleasurable. There are two great pleasures in life that I am grateful for: a strong martini and a great vibrator.

That insight aside, I reassured my companion that although she did not use her best judgment on the previous evening, she was the stronger of the two. She sent him packing, which a lesser woman

might not have done. I also reminded her that she was not solely responsible. This good friend has some serious issues to deal with and having an affair is not a solution. The greatest insight of the evening actually came from the bartender, who had become a welcome participant in the conversation. "It is obvious," he said, "This guy doesn't have any respect for you and even less for his wife, and absolutely none for himself!" You have to love it when a guy calls another guy on his shit! When he said this, the light bulb went on in both our heads.

Conclusion:

We walked home, arm in arm, satisfied after several martinis and a fantastic dinner. We concluded that the bartender was right. She had a lot more respect for herself than she realized; consequently, from that point forward, she would associate with people that honored that respect. Needless to say, the screwed up married guy just never understood why his phone calls have never been returned. This Dilemma will never be revisited, but the Dilemma martini certainly will.

"As long as the Martini tastes
like candy and looks pretty,
I'll drink it"

Emily Ng
Hairstylist

The Dilemma Martini

Recipe:

2 oz. Gin

½ oz. Grand Marnier

½ oz. orange juice

Splash of fresh lime and lemon

Shake with cracked ice and pour into a chilled martini glass.

Garnish with a lime wedge.

This evening was all about drinking, because it was the conclusion to a great day of rednecking with the boys. Boys and toys! We all know that one of the differences between men and boys is the price of their toys. The great thing about aging is that the toys get more expensive, but they are also a hell of lot more fun. With age, the cocktails also get classier and they definitely taste better.

The toy of choice was my buddy's brand new H2 Hummer and the cocktail of choice was, of course, the Hummer martini. Just like the suv slogan, both of the Hummers are "Like nothing else!" There are three consistent things in a man's world: one is the desire to redneck, two is the desire to get laid and the third is the desire for a really good martini. It was this third desire that inspired the consumption of the Hummer martini. This martini is a mixture of Vodka, Grand Marnier and Tequila, with a splash of lime cordial. This combination gives you a martini that has a mean and nasty edge but finishes off sweet and pleasurable.

There is something about a really tough and nasty truck that gets every man's testosterone level raging! Men can sit and discuss the details of a tough truck for hours. Not unlike women who discuss a great shoe sale, or the latest hairstyle that they just got. The Hummer has the stereotype of being the "Pavement princess" - the excessive and expensive SUV that never gets dirty. Unfortunately, this stereotype is true. We razzed my buddy big time for buying the Hummer. The jokes were endless. Was he ever going to get it dirty? What happened if something got spilled inside? Was the truck an extension for what was lacking in his pants? But even though he was the butt of all the jokes, he already had bought it. This day of rednecking was his way of proving to all of us exactly why he had bought the Hummer.

When the boys go rednecking they drink, and drink a lot. I was brought along for the simple purpose of being entertaining eye candy and for my ability to make a great Hummer martini. Beer would have been a lot easier, but not nearly as classy. The dirtier the Hummer got, the more I worked the shaker. The boys were very impressed by what the Hummer could do and the fact that it was both dirty and scratched. While martinis were being poured inside and the H2 was parked and dirty in the driveway, the conversation about "Hummers" moved from the vehicle to the other "Hummer."

"The Hummer is not just a Hummer"

it can mean a blowjob or a blowie - it can refer to giving head. The best phrase was from my buddy, who referred to his girlfriend's time of the month as "Hummer season." The boys laughed hysterically at that one. Why is it that when a woman has her time of the month, the expectation is that the man should get a Hummer? When I asked my buddy what time of the month was Muff Diving season? He seemed perplexed! But what did I expect? After all, he is a redneck. It was interesting to listen to how much a man loves a Hummer, and it was also interesting to hear how few women they had encountered that

actually seemed to enjoy providing this pleasure.

The key ingredients to a great Hummer (all women pay attention) seemed to be the right combination of pressure, suction and lubrication. But the most important component was the rhythm. I could not believe I was having this conversation with a room full of straight men; I have had this conversation before, but only with my gay friends. So this was a completely different perspective. The most fascinating part of this conversation was they all agreed, the most exciting part of a Hummer was when a woman swallowed. The swallow was dirty and nasty, but it was also the most exciting. To a man it was like having the biggest ego stroke ever. What was interesting was how rarely women swallowed. When I surveyed the room, most men said that only about 20% of the women they had been with swallowed. I was shocked, speechless actually. Why do women not get this? If a woman expects to receive pleasure from a man, she must also learn to give pleasure. And shouldn't pleasuring your partner be enjoyable? Why do women despise the Hummer so much? The big question is, why do women use it as leverage to get what they want? Or, why do women use it as a way of getting out of having sex? If the Hummer is something that brings men such pleasure, why is it that women consider it dirty and degrading? Something that brings your partner such pleasure should never be used as a way to control him, and it should never be rationed out like a treat if he has been good. If a woman gives a man a Hummer with the intention of providing her partner with the ultimate pleasure, then this action should never be considered submissive or degrading. It should be thought of as an act of beauty. It goes without saying though that women, if they so desire, deserve the same consideration from their partners.

Conclusion:

The Hummer H2 is a vehicle that is excessive and outrageous. The Hummer martini is exactly the same. This martini has a nasty and exciting edge that comes from the Vodka and Tequila, but the sweetness of the Grand Marnier and lime gives you a finish that is nothing but sheer enjoyment. Satisfying your partner is one of the greatest gifts that a person can give. Both men and women should take pride in being able to give their partners ultimate pleasure. When a woman can give a Hummer and fulfill her man with such an amazing ego stroke, she will learn that it is never dirty. It is just like the H2; hummers are never dirty, they are all a thing of beauty. The Hummer martini is truly "Like nothing else."

"A good Martini is like a woman's favorite black cocktail dress, neither one ever goes out of style"

Fiona Burke
Costume Designer

The Hummer Martini

Recipe:

1 oz. Vodka

½ oz. Grand Marnier

½ oz. Tequila

Splash of Lime Cordial

Salt the rim of a chilled martini glass.

Shake the ingredients with ice and pour into a chilled martini glass.

Garnish with an orange twist.

As always, insight comes to me in the latest hour of the evening. In this case, it was morning due to the extra amount of espresso that was consumed. The Nasty martini is every coffee drinker's dream, and a lovely fantasy it is. It is a combination of espresso, Vanilla Vodka, Bailey's and Kahlua. This martini is shaken and then garnished with chocolate shavings for just the right amount of sweetness. A vibrant, hilarious, and outrageous woman introduced me to the Nasty martini one evening. She had me laughing so hard that my abs got a workout they hadn't seen in years. This very funny woman had just started drinking martinis, because she decided that she drank regular cocktails too quickly. A martini, she could sip and therefore slow her consumption. Whatever the reason, I was glad to see her enjoying my favorite beverage. As I had my first sip of the Nasty martini, I savored the sweetness of the chocolate mixed with Kahlua. I had the feeling that I had just bitten into the best piece of tiramisu ever! The espresso added the bitterness needed to make it not too rich, but very intriguing.

After a few Nasty martinis our conversation turned to

"Our craziest sexual experiences!"

(Now boys control yourselves, you only get to hear one experience.) She retold the story of an interesting night, where after several cocktails, this woman found herself in the delightful company of two handsome and incredibly hot men. She was having a great time talking with these intelligent and witty men. Inevitably, the subject of the "threesome" came up. At first this woman was insulted and shocked; she had never even considered a threesome. That was Yucky!!!

As the conversation continued, she felt like she had a bolt of lightning hit her. "Why not?" She was in her mid thirties and single. These men appeared normal and nice; they didn't seem weird or kinky. The selling feature was she would never see them again! Bonus!!! Besides, she had heard about threesomes, but they were usually with two women and one man, not the other way around. After this conclusion you can only imagine what happened: the hot men got so lucky!

As she walked home in the early hours of the morning, she had a few more revelations. For all the talk around threesomes, it's just that; "talk." The sex was really not that good. Great sex the first time around is pretty much a miracle, let alone with two guys you don't know. The reason she participated was out of curiosity, something to check off of her life experience list. Would she trade a threesome for a long-term lover? Not in a million years, but as she walked home she giggled out loud as she thought, "Wait until the girls hear this one!"

Conclusion:

Like the Nasty Martini, life is always filled with unexpected opportunities. If you are awake enough from the shot of espresso, then you will not miss out. A sexual threesome, can start off sweet and smooth but remember that anything you do sexually that may lower your self esteem, is similar to the bitterness of the espresso, leaving you with a bad taste in your mouth.

If you can walk away and be happy with your experience, and be satisfied that you tried something new, then Game on, girls! But remember to pick your partners carefully and always trust your intuition. Oh yeah ladies, getting back to my girlfriend's story about the threesome… what they say about "some" men is true!!! And men, just so you know, size really does matter!!!

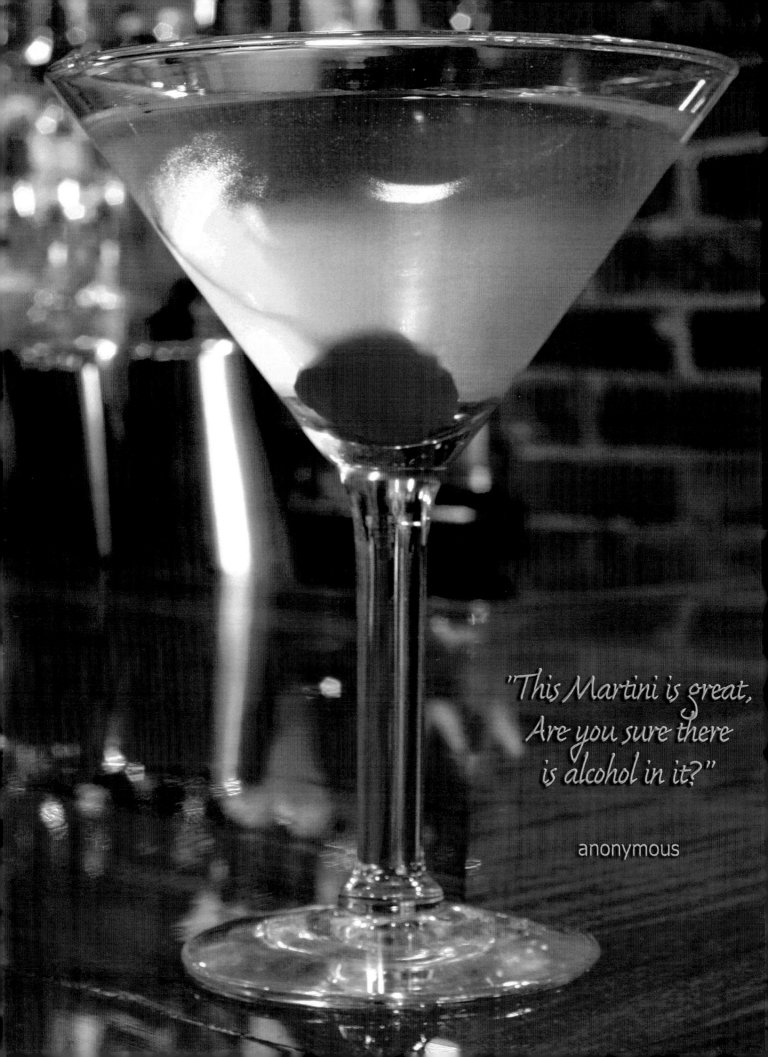

"This Martini is great,
Are you sure there
is alcohol in it?"

anonymous

The Nasty Martini

Recipe:

1 oz. Vanilla Vodka

1 shot of espresso

½ oz. Bailey's

½ oz. Kahlua

Rim a martini glass with cocoa powder.

Shake ingredients and pour into a room temperature martini glass.

Garnish with chocolate shavings.

*O*n this evening the insight was brought to me by a dear friend. We both share several similarities, one of which is our desire for an excellent martini. We were roosting on our favorite bar stools comparing our addiction to the wrong lover but also our desire for an incredible martini. The Addiction martini is one that you absolutely can not say "No" to. It is a martini that when the bartender asks you if you want another you have to say "Yes." It is a martini that gets you all fired up, makes you crazy and one that you can't stop drinking. It has a desire to please all its own.

The Addiction martini is a pleasurable blend of white rum, coconut rum, and banana liqueur, shaken with fresh pineapple juice. This is a martini that may sound a little sweet but is a surprising mixture of flavors, smoothness and sin. It is delusional, because it seems you have only consumed one. This martini is the epitome of "when it is good, it is soooo good and when it is bad, oh god, it is bad." Compare it to an addictive relationship: even though you know, you should get out, it just feels way too great to say "No!"

Addictive relationships, AAAAHHHHH they are the nemesis of many people in this world. What is it about being with someone that can make you feel good but then you can feel very very bad? How does it happen that when you meet someone, it can be incredible in the beginning? The lust combined with the sex, makes you want to be with this person every waking moment? When they are happy it is excellent! Being with them is like the best drug ever, they bring you to incredible highs of laughter, and they drive you crazy with the insatiable sex. All you want to do is be with this person because you are addicted; you just can not get enough of them.

"The Addiction is so strong that you crave those moments of uncontrollable giddiness and lustful ecstasy."

But slowly over a period of time, you notice that the ups are infrequent and the downs, well they are becoming increasingly ugly. The moodiness is very subtle but it is occurring more often. It creeps up throughout an evening, so what started out as a nice night ends up in a fight. The mellow Sunday afternoon all of a sudden becomes full of issues, tears and drama about what you are not doing to fulfill the relationship. This is when the addiction becomes destructive.

Slowly you start to think that you have done something wrong. Or maybe you are not good enough for this person. You decide to walk away from this devastating relationship but somehow you end up getting sucked back in. How does this happen? Do we desire an addictive relationship just like we crave drugs and alcohol? Is this something

that we can not break away from? Do we need rehab to escape from a habitual dependence?

Fortunately, there is a way to calm an addiction it is referred to as "Moderation." This is a way of saying that I am not an addict because I only indulge every once in awhile. But that is really a load of crap, because everyone's version of once in awhile is different. So moderation is not a cure but only a band aid solution. We delude ourselves into believing that if we moderate our cravings then we really do not have a habit. It is like the coffee junkies who limit themselves to 2 cups a day, or the cigarette smoker who only smokes after dinner. Are these people practicing moderation or are they closet addicts in denial? This theory can be applied to relationships. The phrases: "Well we are only sleeping together", or "I only call her every once in awhile" have been spoken by our friends. These are the thoughts we tell ourselves when we have broken away from the addiction but are still getting sucked back in by the comfort. This is when the delusion needs an intervention. It is only with help from a friend that we can accept the reality that we are addicted and hopefully make a choice to get over it. It is then, that you can start to find bliss within yourself and not with a person that is emotionally unstable.

Conclusion:

The Addictive martini is a drink that is so damn

good that you can not say "No." When you mix this combination and take a sip, the satisfaction that washes over you from the flavors of pineapple, coconut and banana is complete hedonism. The rum makes your intentions of moderation dissolve in just one martini. Everyone craves something! Whether it is drugs, alcohol or a deadly relationship. Some people live in the world of delusion by pretending they are not habitual because they practice infrequency. It is only when you accept that you are addicted to something that you can truly break free. You will want to end the addiction when there is more destruction than there is gratification. However, if you enjoy the sensations of this incredible martini then I would suggest careful moderation. After all we sometimes need a little bit of something that is sooooo damn good. "Buyer beware!"

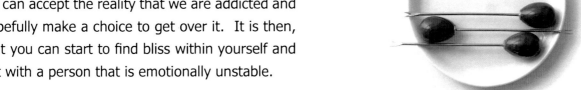

*"A Martini is a
Rich Man's Shooter"*

Anton Fruehwirth
Bartender

The Addiction Martini

Recipe:

1 oz. White Rum

½ oz. Coconut Rum

½ oz. Banana Liqueur

1 oz. pineapple juice

Shake ingredients with cracked ice and strain into a chilled martini glass.

Garnish with a wedge of pineapple.

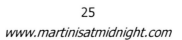

Have you ever heard something that is so unbelievable you walked away completely stunned? I was in a state of bewilderment while I was sitting at my usual martini bar. My buddy, the bartender, commented that "I looked completely perplexed." Well, he had the perfect cure for that, he subsequently created for me the Dazed and Infused martini. This was an evening where I was in shock. I needed this martini to help me process the information that I had just received; somehow it just did not seem possible.

The Dazed and Infused martini is very unique. It requires some serious labor to make this one, but oh boy, it is worth it. A combination of vodka infused with the flavors of vanilla, macadamia nut, cinnamon and topped off with Bailey's. This drink has many flavors, with all the punch, of a pure alcohol martini. Upon visual inspection, I knew that it was going to be impossible not to love this martini, because it was garnished with caramelized sugar. Yum, Yum! When I took my first sip I realized that this martini was one in a million. This was just the drink I needed to clear away my confusion. My taste buds were freaking out, the vanilla and macadamia nut was balanced with the cinnamon so that it was not too sweet, actually luscious. After a few sips, I started to tell my buddy about the source of my confusion. I had just found out about, not one, but two women, who had been in long term sexless relationships, one which was over five years! His response: "What, are you kidding me?" "Yes, it was true!" I replied. The wildest part of the story was that one of these

women had not had sex with her boyfriend for seven years and was still a virgin. Ironically, the boyfriend finally left her for another man.

"So she was 28 years old, single and a virgin!"

Unbelievable! "Let me at her, I will fix that situation in no time," chuckled my bartender. The other woman was in the sexual prime of her mid 30's and had not been sexually active with her boyfriend in five years. The first few years the sex had been fine, but now it had been so long that it was not even discussed. My question was, "How does this happen?"

How does a woman or a man go without sex for so long? Are we not animals? Do we not need sex to survive? Is it not part of our primal instinct? How can you love someone, sleep beside them, be affectionate and not have sex? This is just crazy! I have to question; why would you stay in a relationship if this was happening? Now, I realize that every relationship goes through periods when the sex is minimal - that is only natural. Life factors take over: work stress, children, post pregnancy hormones and over-commitment can leave no time or energy for each other and sex. How does low sex become no sex and how does no sex go on for years?

This woman, who had not had sex for five years, was in a relationship with a man that she loved and cared for. After a few years, it seemed like

every time they kissed and became passionate, he emotionally and physically shut down. They would discuss how they should have sex, but it just did not happen. She had stopped initiating sex because she did not want to be rejected; she felt guilty and unsatisfied when she masturbated because she wanted to have sex instead. Gradually, she started to have feelings of inadequacy and insecurity. She did not feel like a sexual being. The relationship was great on many levels - they were best friends and truly loved each other. Finally, she started seeing a counselor because she thought that she had a problem, but discovered that she was just fine. When her boyfriend started seeing the counselor, he encountered some sexual issues. Well, no kidding! Eventually, this led to the end of their relationship. It was interesting to talk to her, because she thought that she had a low sex drive. However, after leaving this situation and consequently having a healthy sexual relationship, she has realized that she has a very strong sex drive. So do people have a low or high sex drive, or is it that we all have strong sex drives, but they get overshadowed by sexual issues that we have not dealt with?

After discussing this with my bartender and having another Dazed and Infused martini, I came to the conclusion that we are all creatures with the primal instinct to have sex. This is an act that gives us pleasure. So isn't it natural that if we do something that gives us such enjoyment that we would want more and more of it. How many times have you had and orgasm that was so satisfying that afterwards you think, "I really should do this more often!" What happens to us to make us resist our natural instincts? Is it the beliefs with which we were raised, that sex is dirty or bad? Is it that many of us have been sexually molested or abused and this has caused our sexuality to be repressed? Is it that we put so much focus on other areas of our relationships that we undervalue how important sex really is? If this is the case, are we not just living in a state of sexual denial? Are we sexually dazed and confused?

Conclusion:

The Dazed and Infused martini is a drink that you should consume when you are totally perplexed in life. Life is crazy, and it can be enlightening to learn what other people have gone through. With its flavors of vanilla and macadamia nut, this martini can let you sit back and contemplate how unhappy people can be. This martini flows into the sweet flavors of cinnamon and Bailey's. It's a drink that is both delicious and intoxicating. A person's sex drive is not low or high; it is a natural instinct. When you are in a relationship where sex is not important, you are just cheating yourself and your partner. Sex is one of the most important things in a relationship. It's the prime reason men and women bond. The purpose of sex is to bring ourselves ecstasy, it should be sweet and sensual, erotic and addictive, just like the Dazed and Infused martini. Whether you make the attempt to have sex or make the effort to infuse this martini, you will realize that they are both pure bliss.

"Wow, This Martini is Strong"
"Ya, Martini is code word for
straight booze in a pretty glass"

Jack Hurtubise
Retired Bartender

The Dazed and Infused Martini

Recipe:

3 oz. Infused Vodka

¼ oz. Bailey's

To infuse vodka: Combine 26 oz. vodka with roasted vanilla beans,

macadamia nuts and cinnamon. Let sit as long as possible, minimum 48 hours.

Pour ingredients into a shaker with cracked ice and shake well.

Strain into a chilled martini glass.

Garnish with caramelized sugar.

More
Martinis

Apple Martini

Garnish with a cheddar cheese wedge to be different and slightly edgy. For those who can't handle the lactose, use the apple slice slightly salted.

Recipe:

- 1 oz. Green Apple Vodka
- 1 oz. Apple Sour or Apple Puckers

Shake with ice and strain into a chilled martini glass. Salt the rim and garnish with a cheese wedge or apple slice.

Golden Martini

This twist on the original martini switches gin to golden gin. The taste difference is lovely.

Recipe:

- 2 oz. Golden Gin
- ½ oz. Vermouth

Stir over ice and strain into a chilled martini glass. Garnish with a spear of olives.

For a dry martini, omit the Vermouth and garnish with a lemon twist.

Dirty Vodka Martini

This martini is the brother of the dirty gin martini. This is for all of those people who can not drink gin.

Recipe:

- 1 ½ oz. of Vodka

- Hint of Vermouth

- Splash of olive juice

- olives

Stir over ice and strain into a chilled martini glass. Garnish with olives stuffed with Blue cheese, smoked salmon, or anchovies etc. Very yummy.

Brantini Martini

A great combination of gin and brandy. Even if you are not a brandy fan, you will like this one. Good and stiff, just the way a martini should be.

Recipe:

- ½ oz. Brandy
- 1 oz. Gin Faint
- Splash of Dry Vermouth

Shake with ice and strain into a chilled martini glass. Garnish with a lemon twist.

Chocolate Martini

When a woman eats chocolate, the same chemicals in her brain are released as when she has an orgasm. Need I say more.

Recipe:

- 1 oz. Vanilla Vodka
- 1 oz. White Crème de Cacao
- 1 Hershey's kiss
- chocolate/cocoa powder

Shake with ice and strain into a chilled martini glass. Garnish the rim of a glass with chocolate (chocolate will harden if chilled) or cocoa powder and put a Hershey's kiss in bottom of the glass, tip up.

Dirty Gin Martini

This is a nasty version of the original. If you have a love of olives, this drink is for you.

Recipe:

- 1 ½ oz. Gin

- Hint of Vermouth

- Splash of olive juice

- olives

Stir over ice and strain into a chilled martini glass. Garnish with olives, of course!

Ginger Cosmopolitan Martini

A variation of the original; it's a nice way to spice it up and feel like a movie star from Gilligan's Island.

Recipe:

- 2 oz. Ginger Vodka
- 1 oz. Cointreau
- 1 oz. lime juice
- 2 oz. cranberry juice

Shake with ice and strain into a chilled martini glass. Garnish with a lime wedge or lemon twist.

Flirtini Martini

The name explains it all – this martini will enhance your powers over the opposite sex, and damn it's tasty.

Recipe:

- ½ oz. Raspberry Vodka
- ½ oz. Cointreau
- Splash of lime juice, pineapple juice, cranberry juice
- Brut Champagne
- raspberries
- sprig of mint

Put raspberries in the bottom of a chilled martini glass. Shake the first five ingredients and strain into glass. Top with champagne and garnish with a sprig of mint.

Cosmopolitan Martini

This is the original ladies drink, nice and tart.

Women feel sexy after a few.

Recipe:

- 2 oz. Citron Vodka

- 1 oz. Cointreau

- 1 oz. lime juice (fresh)

- 2 oz. cranberry juice

Shake with ice and strain into a chilled martini

glass. Garnish with a lime wedge.

Emerald Martini

A very light and refreshing martini; for those who want something a little different.

Recipe:

- 1 ½ oz. Gin

- ½ oz. Vermouth

- Dash of Chartreuse Green Liqueur

- orange twist

Stir over ice and strain into a chilled martini glass. Garnish with an orange twist.

Key Lime Martini

Recipe:

- 2 oz Vodka

- 1/4 oz Lemon Liqueur

- 1/2 oz Key Lime Liqueur

- 1 oz half and half cream

Pour ingredients with crushed ice into shaker and let stand for five seconds. Shake vigorously for five seconds. Strain into chilled martini glass. Garnish with a slice of lime.

Crantini Martini

Recipe:

- 2 oz Vodka

- 2 ¾ oz cranberry juice

- 1/3 oz lime cordial

Pour ingredients into a shaker with cracked ice and shake well. Strain into chilled martini glasses. Garnish with a lime wedge.

Breakfast Martini

One of the only hangover cures that actually works.

Recipe:

- 2 oz. Gin
- ½ oz. Triple Sec
- 1 oz. Clamato juice
- celery salt
- tomato wedge
- celery stick

Stir over ice and strain into a martini glass rimmed with celery salt. Garnish with a celery stick and tomato wedge.

Lemon Drop Martini

One of my very favorite martinis, it is sweet yet tangy and it goes down so smooth.

Recipe:

- 1 ½ oz. Citron Vodka
- Dash of Triple Sec
- lemon wedge
- sugar

Hand swirl over ice and strain into a sugared-rim chilled martini glass. Garnish with a lemon wedge.

Liqueurs Defined

Liqueurs/Ingredients Defined

Bailey's Original Irish Cream: A chocolate flavored cream liqueur made from Irish whiskey, cream and chocolate.

Chambord (Liqueur Royale de France): A very sweet berry flavored liqueur made from small black raspberries, other fruits, herbs and honey. It is dark purple in color.

Chartreuse (Green): An ancient herbal liqueur developed by the Carthusian monks in the early 1600's. It has been commercially produced since 1848. It is pale green in color and refreshing. It is made from a grape brandy base and flavored with 130 herbs and plants. Its sweetness is balanced by the bitterness of the herbs. The green variety is 100 proof.

Cointreau: A strongly flavored orange liqueur. A French liqueur made from brandy and sweet and bitter Mediterranean and tropical orange peels.

Crème de Cacao: A sweet chocolate liqueur made of cocoa beans, vanilla and spices. It is available in brown and white varieties. Some brands are more artificially flavored than others.

Grand Marnier: An orange flavored French liqueur. A cognac base flavored with the peels of bitter wild oranges.

Kahlua: A classic coffee flavored liqueur from Mexico.

Triple Sec: An orange flavored liqueur, made from the Dutch West Indies orange peel. Rather like Curacao but sweeter and higher proof. It is clear.

Vermouth: A sweet or dry fortified wine flavored with aromatic herbs and used chiefly in mixed drinks.

Drinking Responsibly

Despite more than twenty years of public awareness campaigns and law enforcement efforts, many people are still totally unaware of the dangers surrounding alcohol abuse. Myths abound -- have you ever heard that drinking coffee will "wake up" someone who is drunk? The truth is, only time can neutralize that "buzz." Alcohol abuse is responsible for millions of injuries and deaths each year across the world. Approximately half of all fatal motor vehicle accidents in North America involve alcohol, a number which is rising according to research by traffic authorities.

In 2000, the United States experienced its largest percentage increase in alcohol-related traffic deaths on record. In a recent survey by Nationwide Insurance, 13 percent of adults say that they have driven with someone who has had too much to drink, or they themselves have driven while intoxicated in the past year. Underage and especially binge drinking -- often considered a "rite of passage" -- also remains a very important concern, costing more than $52 billion per year in the USA alone. Studies have shown that young people who drink are more likely to develop drinking or drug problems, be involved in a violent crime and engage in unsafe sexual activity. It's more important than ever for individuals and families to be aware of the facts when it comes to alcohol abuse at all ages.

So keep it real and keep it safe. Don't let friends drive drunk. The cost of a cab home will always be less than the cost of a night's lodging in the emergency ward, or the local police station.

Now with that said, let's get down to the enjoyment of some of the most popular Martinis around...

Acknowledgements

The author would like to offer special thanks to:

Her fabulous girlfriends, for all their support and great ideas. Trust is beautiful, thanks for believing in this project.

All those who helped in the development and tasting of the recipes.

Vally Haeck: Webmaster, the man who started it all, and to Derek Jarman, for being the king martini taster.

Victoria Laan and Diane Hart, who painstakingly edited and formatted every word in their unwavering commitment to make it perfect.

Kelley Laan, the creative genius who designed all the graphics and the book cover. Words can not describe your incredible support of this dream.

Special thanks to my favorite bartenders Jack Hurtubise, Wayne Escott and Anton Fruehwirth.